Jenny Archer to the Rescue

	DATE DUE	

ܛܘܒ ܕܚܝܠܐ ܀

Jenny Archer to the Rescue

by Ellen Conford

Illustrated by Diane Palmisciano

Little, Brown and Company

Boston   New York   Toronto   London

First Paperback Edition

The characters and events in this book are fictitious.
Any similarity to real persons, living or dead, is
coincidental and not intended by the author.

Library of Congress Cataloging-in-Publication Data

Conford, Ellen.
    Jenny Archer to the rescue / by Ellen Conford: illustrated by
Diane Palmisciano. — 1st ed.
    p.   cm. (Springboard books)
    Summary: After perfecting her first aid skills, Jenny is disappointed
in not finding anyone to rescue and decides to invent her own
emergencies.
    ISBN 0-316-15351-6 (hc)
    ISBN 0-316-15369-9 (pb)
    [1. First aid — Fiction.   2. Humorous stories.]
I. Palmisciano, Diane, ill.   II. Title.
PZ7.C7593Jg   1990
[Fic] — dc20   90-36190

Springboard Books and design is a registered trademark of
Little, Brown and Company (Inc.)

10 9 8 7 6 5 4 3 2

WOR

*Published simultaneously in Canada
by Little, Brown & Company (Canada) Limited*

Printed in the United States of America

Jenny Archer
to the Rescue

1

Jenny Archer was reading her favorite newspaper, *Kid Talk*. She lay on the living room floor, resting her head on her dog, Barkley.

On the front page of *Kid Talk* there was a photo of a girl about Jenny's age. She wore a big gold medal on a ribbon around her neck.

The president of the United States was shaking her hand. The headline said:

YOUNG AMERICAN HEROES —
THE BRAVEST KIDS IN THE COUNTRY.

"Wow," said Jenny. "The president."
She read the story underneath the headline:

> Tracy Tibbets saved her brother Eric from drowning. Eric fell through the ice on a frozen pond last winter. Quick-thinking, brave Tracy saved his life. She jumped into the pond after her brother. She swam under the ice and pulled Eric to safety.

Jenny turned the page. On the second page there were more photos of Young American Heroes. There was a seven-year-old boy who saved his family when their house burned down.

There was a ten-year-old girl who carried her sister for three miles to a hospital. The sister had been bitten by a snake while they were on a picnic.

"Three miles!" said Jenny. Barkley yawned.

On the same page there was a quiz: "*Do*

you know what to do in an emergency?"
Jenny got a pencil. She began testing herself.

> *What do you do if:*
> Someone is hit by a car?
> Someone stops breathing?
> Someone is bleeding?
> Someone gets bitten by a snake?

Jenny chewed the end of her pencil. She pushed her glasses higher on her nose. "I'm not doing very well on this test," she told Barkley. He snored softly.

There were ten questions. For most of her answers Jenny wrote, "Call 911."

But what if you weren't near a phone?

When she finished the quiz, she checked her answers. She scored only thirty points out of a hundred.

I don't know one thing about saving people, she thought. I'd better not have any emergencies.

But she looked at the photos of the Young

American Heroes. She read what the president said to them in his speech.

How proud they must be, she thought. And famous, too.

She wondered how it would feel to get a gold medal from the president of the United States. She closed her eyes. She could almost see herself shaking hands with the president. She could see her parents, beaming with pride.

It would be the greatest moment of her whole life.

There was only one problem.

How could she be a hero if she didn't know how to rescue anyone?

2

Jenny's parents were in the kitchen drinking coffee.

"Do we have a first aid kit?" Jenny asked.

"No, we don't," said her mother.

"Don't you think we should have one?" Jenny asked.

"Yes," said her father. "We should. I'll pick one up tomorrow on the way home."

"We have a booklet on first aid," said Mrs. Archer. "I think it's in the bookcase in the living room."

"Good," said Jenny. "I'll start reading it."

"Why?"

Jenny showed her mother the story in *Kid Talk*. She showed her parents the bad mark she'd gotten on the quiz.

"I could never rescue anybody," she said. "I might not even be able to rescue myself."

"Let me have that booklet when you're finished, Jenny," her mother said. "I want to read it, too."

"You don't have to," Jenny said. "I'm going to learn it all."

Her mother smiled. "But what if we need first aid when you're not around?"

"I hope that doesn't happen," said Jenny. It would be terrible if her parents had an emergency when she wasn't there to save them.

Jenny found the first aid booklet and began to read. She was amazed at all the accidents that could happen to people. It was a little scary.

But I won't be scared, she told herself. I'm going to be a hero. And heroes don't get scared.

The next morning Jenny read the booklet again while she ate her cereal.

"You're going to be a real expert," her father said.

"I hope so," said Jenny. "Don't forget to buy the first aid kit."

Jenny met her friends Wilson Wynn and Beth Moore on the corner of Lemon Street. Beth was in Jenny's class at school. Wilson was a year younger.

"Did you do the arithmetic homework?" Beth asked.

"Uh oh," Jenny said. "I was reading. I forgot all about it."

"Did you finish your book for the oral report?" Beth asked.

"Uh oh," said Jenny. "I wasn't reading that

book." She pulled the first aid booklet out of her folder. "I was reading about what to do in an emergency."

"Does it tell you what to do if you have a homework emergency?" asked Wilson.

Jenny shook her head. "That must be the only emergency that isn't in the book."

Before class started, Jenny was able to do a few arithmetic problems. When it was time for arithmetic, Mrs. Pike asked Jenny to do an example on the chalkboard.

Jenny was lucky. It was one of the problems she had done.

The oral reports started at two-thirty. Jenny was sure Mrs. Pike wouldn't call on her. After all, she had already done an arithmetic problem. And there were twenty other kids to call on.

Just before three o'clock, Mrs. Pike said, "We can listen to one more report." She looked around the room.

Jenny kept her head down and tried to be invisible.

"Jenny," said the teacher, "let's hear about your book."

Uh oh.

"Come to the front," said Mrs. Pike.

"Well," Jenny started, "I didn't exactly —"

"Didn't you read a book?"

"Yes, I did," said Jenny. "But —"

Suddenly Jenny knew what to do. She took the first aid booklet from her notebook. She walked to the front of the room.

"This is the book I read." She held up the booklet for everyone to see. "I read it twice," she said. "It's a very important book."

She showed the title to Mrs. Pike.

"I know it's not on our book list," said Jenny. "But if you read this you could save someone's life."

"What a good idea for a book report,"

Mrs. Pike said. "Tell us what you learned, Jenny."

So Jenny told the class how to make a cut stop bleeding. She told them how to tie a splint to a broken bone. She told them what to do if someone gets an electric shock.

Mrs. Pike smiled warmly. Jenny could tell that her teacher was very interested in her report.

"Wait till you hear what you have to do for snakebite," Jenny told the class.

The bell rang.

"It's really disgusting."

3
_____

Jenny met her father at the door.

"Did you get the first aid kit?"

"May I come inside first?" he asked.

"Did you get it?"

"Yes." He handed Jenny a large plastic
bag. Inside was a metal box a little larger than
her lunch box. It was white and had a red
cross on it.

She opened the box. "Wow! This has every-
thing the booklet said we needed." There
were Band-Aids and bandages. There was a

small bottle of peroxide and a box of aspirin. A tube of Vaseline and cotton balls. And a package of wooden tongue depressors.

"This is great!" Jenny said.

"I hope we never have to use it," said her father.

"Really?" Jenny asked. She could hardly wait for her first emergency.

Things were very quiet at the Archer house that night. Mr. and Mrs. Archer watched television. Jenny watched with them. But she watched her parents more than she watched TV.

Barkley slept under the coffee table. Jenny checked under the table a few times, just to make sure Barkley was okay.

"Do we ever get tornadoes here?" she asked.

"No," said her mother.

"Is there a pond to ice-skate on?" she asked.

"There's the skating rink at the park," her mother said. "But it's May."

"You can't fall through the ice at a skating rink," Jenny said glumly.

"Especially not in May," her father said.

"What about bears?" asked Jenny.

"Bears?"

"Do we have any woods here? Where bears might be?"

"Jenny, there are no bears in this neighborhood," her father said. "There are no woods in this neighborhood."

"You sound as if you really want a disaster to happen," her mother said.

"Well, what's the point of knowing how to rescue someone," said Jenny, "if you never have anyone to rescue?"

Just before Jenny went to bed that night, she fed Phyllis, her big goldfish. Phyllis nibbled at the food. She swam around the bowl, swishing her tail.

She looked very healthy. And she certainly wasn't going to drown.

It's just as well, thought Jenny. After all, how could you do mouth-to-mouth breathing with a fish?

4

The next day Jenny took the first aid kit to school.

"Why did you bring two lunch boxes?" asked Wilson.

"This isn't a lunch box." She opened the kit and showed it to them.

"That's neat!" said Beth.

"It's like a doctor kit," said Wilson. "I have a doctor kit."

"This isn't a toy," said Jenny. "This is all real first aid stuff."

When she got to her classroom, Jenny put her lunch box and the first aid kit inside her desk.

Mrs. Pike started to write arithmetic problems on the chalkboard.

Suddenly there was a snapping sound. Mrs. Pike said, "Ouch."

Jenny grabbed the first aid kit. In a flash she got to the front of the room.

"Don't worry, Mrs. Pike," she said. "I know how to put a splint on a broken finger."

"Thank you, Jenny," said Mrs. Pike. "But my finger is fine. The chalk broke. I just bent my fingernail backwards."

"Maybe we should spray some Bactine on it," Jenny said hopefully. "I have some in my kit."

I don't think I need Bactine," said the teacher.

"I could put a Band-Aid on it," Jenny said. "So it doesn't bend back again."

"I don't need a Band-Aid," said Mrs. Pike.

22

"Look." She held out her finger.

Jenny looked at it. It looked perfectly okay.

"Please take your seat, Jenny," Mrs. Pike said. "And let's open our workbooks to page forty-five."

Jenny walked back to her desk. She put the first aid kit away. She was glad Mrs. Pike wasn't really hurt.

But how long would it be before she got to rescue someone?

5

On Saturday afternoon Jenny took Barkley out for a walk. Barkley was a very good dog. Jenny had trained him herself, with a little help from her father.

Across the street, Mrs. Katz was just coming outside. She had her little dog, Kiss Kiss, on a leash. Kiss Kiss was really Mr. Katz's dog. But sometimes Mrs. Katz had to walk her.

Mrs. Katz was hardly down her front steps before she started grumbling at Kiss Kiss.

"Don't pull so hard!" She yanked on Kiss Kiss's leash. Kiss Kiss ran in a circle around Mrs. Katz, winding the leash around her ankles.

"Stop tripping me!" Mrs. Katz turned around and around, trying to unwind the leash.

Suddenly Kiss Kiss scooted between her feet. Mrs. Katz dropped the leash. Kiss Kiss headed down the street on the run. The leash trailed behind her.

"Stupid dog!" yelled Mrs. Katz.

Barkley watched as Kiss Kiss raced away. He looked at Jenny and panted. He wanted to chase Kiss Kiss, but he knew he wasn't supposed to.

"Don't worry, Mrs. Katz!" Jenny shouted. "We'll save Kiss Kiss."

"Don't do me any favors!" yelled Mrs. Katz.

Barkley wiggled with excitement. "Okay, Barkley," said Jenny. "Fetch Kiss Kiss!"

26

Barkley nearly flew down the street after Kiss Kiss. Jenny followed him.

Kiss Kiss ran over the hose on Mr. Daley's lawn. Barkley followed her right through the sprinkler.

The little dog ran across the street, toward Beth's house. A large truck was parked in front. Two men came out of the truck. Each man was holding up the end of a large couch.

Kiss Kiss scooted underneath the couch the men were carrying and kept on running. The delivery men put the couch down on the sidewalk so they could rest. Barkley jumped onto the couch. He scrambled over the top and jumped off the other side. He left muddy pawprints all over it.

The delivery men began to scream.

Beth leaned out her window. "What's going on?"

"You're getting a new couch," Jenny called back. "But I don't think your mother will like it."

Barkley and Kiss Kiss turned the corner of Lemon Street. Jenny ran after them. Kiss Kiss ran behind Mr. Munch's house. Barkley ran after her.

Jenny was out of breath when she caught up with them.

Mr. Munch was in the yard. He was standing next to a barbecue grill. He had a large spoon in his hand. On the shelf next to the grill was a broken jar. Red sauce was dripping onto the ground.

Kiss Kiss ran in circles around Mr. Munch. Barbecue sauce was spattered all over her white fur. Barkley had barbecue sauce all over his black fur.

Mr. Munch's apron looked like a finger-painting.

"Why are these dogs in my yard?" he asked. "Why are you in my yard? Why is there barbecue sauce all over me?"

"I'm sorry, Mr. Munch," said Jenny. "I had to save Kiss Kiss."

Mr. Munch frowned. "Save her from what?"

"She was running away. I'm sorry about the mess."

"Luckily I have another jar of barbecue sauce," he said.

"I hope you have another apron," Jenny said.

Mr. Munch finally smiled. "Mrs. Katz will be pretty surprised when you bring Kiss Kiss back."

"I guess she will," Jenny said. The dog was a mess. She had red stains on her head. Her paws were muddy. She was soaking wet.

But the important thing is, we rescued her, Jenny thought. She walked back to Mrs. Katz's house.

She rang the doorbell.

Mrs. Katz came to the screen door.

"We saved her, Mrs. Katz!" Jenny held up the dog. "We brought her back."

Mrs. Katz didn't even open the door. She turned around and yelled into the house.

"Elliot! Your stupid dog is home!"

6

The next week Jenny took her first aid kit to school every single day. But no one got cut. No one got burned. No one got bitten by a snake. Beth tripped on the stairs, but other than that, things were very quiet at school.

On Sunday Jenny and her parents went to visit Uncle Paul and Aunt Marian. Whenever they visited, Jenny took care of her cousin Suzy.

Suzy was two years old. She was always

getting into trouble. When she was only one, she jumped up and down in her crib until it fell over. Once she broke Phyllis's goldfish bowl, and Phyllis nearly died.

Suzy colored in Jenny's stamp album. She pulled the heads off Jenny's dinosaur models. She tried to feed Barkley Play-Doh.

Suzy was sure to do something dangerous while they were there.

Jenny took the first aid kit along.

Suzy was all dressed up when they got to the house.

"How pretty you look, Suzy," said Mrs. Archer.

Suzy twirled around in a circle. "Suzy pretty," she said.

"Is that a new dress?" asked Jenny.

"She wanted to wear it for company," said Uncle Paul.

"She promised not to get dirty," said Aunt Marian.

"I give her five minutes," Uncle Paul whispered to Jenny.

Suzy twirled around again. "Not dirty," she said.

"Don't worry," said Jenny. "I won't take my eyes off her."

Suzy took Jenny's hand. She led her into her room. "Play with Suzy," she said.

"Okay. What do you want to play?"

"Patty-cake," Suzy said.

"Okay." Jenny held up her hands. Suzy held up her hands. "Patty-cake, patty-cake, baker's man."

"Bake! Cake! Fast! Can!" Suzy said.

When they finished, Suzy clapped her hands. "Again!"

"Okay, okay!" Jenny held up her hands again. "Patty-cake, patty-cake . . ."

After ten minutes of patty-cake, Jenny's arms were getting tired.

"No more patty-cake," she said.

34

Suzy climbed off her bed. She took a book from her toy box.

"Read me," she said.

Jenny opened the book. Before she could read the words, Suzy shouted them out. All Jenny did was turn the pages.

"Again!" Suzy said when they finished the book.

"Oh, no!" said Jenny.

"*Again!*"

Jenny read the book two more times. What a boring day, she thought. Suzy wasn't going to get into any trouble. She hadn't even gotten dirty.

Then Jenny got an idea. "Let's go outside, Suzy," she said. "I just thought of a new game. It's called Accident."

7

Jenny got the first aid kit from the car. She and Suzy went into the backyard.

"I'm going to practice first aid on you," Jenny said. "That way I'll be ready for a real emergency." Jenny opened the first aid kit.

"Let's pretend you fell out of a tree," she said.

"No!" said Suzy. "Don't want to fall."

"It's just a game," Jenny said. "Pretend you broke your arm." She held Suzy's arm straight with a tongue depressor. She wrapped a bandage around it.

"See?" said Jenny. "That's a splint."

Suzy looked at her arm. "More!" She forgot about her new dress. Jenny forgot about her new dress.

"Okay." Jenny took an elastic bandage and wound it around Suzy's ankle. "This is what you do for a sprained ankle," she said.

Suzy was so little that the bandage went all the way up her leg.

"More!" said Suzy.

"You're a very good patient," Jenny said. "Here's what I would do if you were bleeding." She pressed a big square of cloth against Suzy's other arm. She tied it on with a long strip of gauze.

"And you hurt your head." Jenny dabbed Mercurochrome on Suzy's forehead. "You're also in shock. I'll get a blanket."

"Blanket!" said Suzy.

"We have one in the car," Jenny said. "I'll be right back. Don't move!"

She was sure Suzy couldn't move, even if she wanted to. She had too many bandages on.

Jenny ran into the house. "I need the car keys," she said to her parents. "I want to get a blanket from the trunk."

"Having a picnic?" Uncle Paul asked.

"Not exactly."

Jenny hurried to the car and got out the blanket. She ran back to the yard.

"Oh, no!"

Suzy had the whole roll of bandage tangled around her. She looked like a mummy. She had spilled Mercurochrome all over her dress. She was chewing a Band-Aid. Bottles and tubes were scattered all around her.

"I told you not to move!" Jenny wailed.

Just then Aunt Marian and Jenny's parents looked out the back door.

Aunt Marian screamed. "What are you doing?"

She ran out the door and grabbed Suzy.

"Accident!" said Suzy.

"Not a real accident," Jenny said. "It was just a game."

"How did she get like this?" Jenny's mother asked.

"I only left her alone for a second," Jenny said.

Her father looked very angry. "You left a two-year-old baby alone with a first aid kit?"

"I'm sorry," Jenny said.

"From now on," her father said, "that kit is off limits to you."

Jenny felt terrible. She knew she was wrong to leave Suzy alone. She understood why her father was angry. But he didn't have to tell her not to use the first aid kit anymore.

There was hardly any first aid kit left.

8

All the next week Jenny looked for chances to save people. Even without a first aid kit, she might be able to rescue someone.

But the worker on the telephone pole didn't fall off. And the man fixing the electric lines didn't get a shock.

Kiss Kiss ran away again, but Jenny stayed inside the house and watched her from the window.

I will never be a Young American Hero, she thought sadly.

When Jenny got home from school on Thursday afternoon, Mrs. Butterfield was waiting for her. Mrs. Butterfield was Jenny's person-sitter. Jenny felt she was too old to have a baby-sitter.

"Your mother will be late from work," Mrs. Butterfield said, "and Barkley needs a walk."

Barkley ran to get his leash. Jenny clipped it to his collar.

"We'll have milk and cookies when you get back," Mrs. Butterfield said.

"This is going to be a short walk," Jenny told Barkley. They started down the street. Jenny was thinking about being a hero — and how she would never be one.

Suddenly she smelled something. It smelled like —

Smoke! Jenny looked down the street. Puffs of black smoke blew over the Katz's roof.

"Fire!" she yelled.

42

She dropped Barkley's leash. She ran back to her house. Barkley ran after her.

"Fire!" she yelled. "Call the fire department!"

"Where?" asked Mrs. Butterfield.

Jenny pulled her outside. "See?" The smoke was thicker now.

"You're right!" Mrs. Butterfield hurried to the phone. She dialed 911.

"I'm going to make sure there's no one in the house," Jenny said.

"Don't you go in there!" Mrs. Butterfield ordered.

"I won't. I'll just yell."

"Fire!" Mrs. Butterfield shouted into the phone. "1716 Lemon Street. Hurry!"

Jenny ran outside. Mrs. Butterfield dropped the phone. She ran out the door after Jenny. "Be careful!"

"I will!"

This is it! Jenny thought. I'm going to rescue Mrs. Katz. I *am* going to be a hero!

"Fire!" Jenny ran toward the house. "Mrs. Katz! Your house is on fire!" She pounded on the door.

"Get away from the house!" Mrs. Butterfield cried, running after Jenny.

Jenny heard a siren. It sounded far away. She saw smoke puffing over the roof. But she didn't see any flames.

She ran to the backyard. Then she stopped short.

Mrs. Katz was standing next to a pile of burning rubbish.

"Uh oh," said Jenny. "I thought your house was on fire."

"I'm just burning some trash," Mrs. Katz said.

"We called the fire department," Jenny said as Mrs. Butterfield joined her.

"I guess you'd better call them back." Mrs. Katz poked at the fire with a rake.

The sirens got louder.

"Too late," said Mrs. Katz. She smiled. She thought it was funny. At least she wasn't angry.

Jenny could hear shouting and clanging from the street. The sirens screamed and suddenly stopped.

Jenny wished she could run home and hide.

9

Mrs. Butterfield took Jenny's hand. They walked to the front of the house. All over Lemon Street, people were running toward them.

Even Wilson's mother was there. She hurried down the street, holding Wilson's baby brother, Tyler. Wilson ran ahead of her. Beth ran out of her house and followed Wilson.

Three fire engines were stopped in front of Mrs. Katz's house. "Where's the fire?" asked one of the firefighters.

"It was a mistake," Jenny said. But she didn't say it very loudly.

Another firefighter pointed toward the smoke. "Look! There it is!" Two of them grabbed the coil of hose. They raced to the backyard.

"This is the most embarrassing thing that ever happened to me," said Jenny.

"It's not your fault," said Mrs. Butterfield. "I thought there was a fire, too."

The firefighters came back, pulling the hose after them. Mrs. Katz followed them to the street.

"It's against the law," one of the firefighters said.

"Can't I burn some trash in my own backyard?" she asked.

"No," said the firefighter. "You have to take the trash to the dump or bag it so the garbage collectors will take it."

"Well, what are you going to do to me?" Mrs. Katz laughed. "Throw me in jail?"

"No," said the firefighter. "We're going to give you a summons. You'll have to pay a fifty-dollar fine."

"Fifty dollars!" Mrs. Katz began to get red in the face.

"Uh oh," said Jenny.

"Let's get out of here," Mrs. Butterfield whispered. She took Jenny's hand.

This is absolutely the last time I try to rescue anyone, Jenny promised herself. Being a hero is too dangerous around here.

10

Even Mrs. Butterfield's homemade sugar cookies couldn't cheer Jenny up.

"The new issue of *Kid Talk* came in the mail today," said Mrs. Butterfield, hoping to make her feel better.

"I hope it doesn't give me any more great ideas," Jenny said.

Mrs. Butterfield turned on the TV. Jenny sat down on the rug to read the newspaper. Barkley lay down next to her.

On the front page there was a photo of a

boy holding a test tube. The headline said:

BOY SCIENTIST
DISCOVERS CURE FOR WARTS.

"Wow," said Jenny. "He's only two years older than me."

She began to read the story under the photo.

> Lionel Felder was only nine years old when he got his first chemistry set.

"A year younger than me," Jenny told Barkley. He licked her nose.

> Right away Lionel's parents knew that their son had a special gift. Soon Lionel was doing experiments every day in the Felders' basement.

"We have a basement," Jenny said.

> "He did have a few explosions," says Mrs. Felder, "but it was all in the name of science."

The wart cure is not the only medicine Lionel has invented. Last year he came up with a pimple cream for teenagers and a cough syrup for dogs.

"How about that, Barkley?" Jenny patted his head. Barkley didn't cough much, but she knew dogs could catch colds.

"This is amazing." She was so interested in the article that she forgot all about Mrs. Katz's fire.

Lionel Felder would probably become a famous scientist. He would invent cures for terrible diseases. He would help people all over the world.

He might even win the Nobel Prize!

When Jenny's mother came home, Mrs. Butterfield told her what had happened that afternoon.

"You were right to call the fire department," said Mrs. Archer. "If the house was on fire, you really would have been a hero."

"Maybe," said Jenny. "But I've decided I don't want to be a hero anymore."

"I guess that's just as well," Mrs. Archer said gently.

"I'm going to be a scientist," Jenny said.

"What made you decide that?" asked Mrs. Archer.

"A hero only gets to rescue one person," Jenny said. "A scientist can save *millions* of people. A scientist could invent a cure for cancer. And maybe even win the Nobel Prize!"

"I'll be very proud if you become a scientist when you grow up," her mother said. "Even if you don't win the Nobel Prize."

"But I don't have to wait till I grow up," Jenny said. She showed her mother the article about Lionel Felder.

"He's only twelve."

"Then I guess you'd better hurry up and get started," joked Mrs. Archer.

Jenny's eyes were bright with excitement. She could almost see her picture on the first page of *Kid Talk*. The headline would say:

TEN-YEAR-OLD DISCOVERS
CURE FOR CANCER.

"I'm going to start," said Jenny. "I'm going to start right away. Just as soon as you buy me a chemistry set!"